Tower 4
"Another one for the Books"
By Steven Bazydlo

Tower 4 Another one for the Books

Tower 4, Volume 1

Steven Bazydlo

Published by Steven Bazydlo, 2024.

This is a work of fiction. Similarities to real people, places, or events are entirely coincidental.

TOWER 4 ANOTHER ONE FOR THE BOOKS

First edition. November 19, 2024.

Copyright © 2024 Steven Bazydlo.

ISBN: 979-8230299011

Written by Steven Bazydlo.

Table of Contents

7/9/24 1

7/10/24 9

7/11/24 11

7/12/24 15

7/13/24 21

7/14/24 27

7/16/24 31

7/19/24 37

8/1/24 49

8/17/24 57

8/31/24 103

9/1/24 105

Editor: Tasha Schiedel

Cover artist: Matt Seff Barnes

Log Entries 7/9/24-9/1/24

7/9/24
7/10/24
7/11/24
7/12/24
7/13/24
7/14/24
7/16/24
7/19/24
8/1/24
8/17/24
8/31/24
9/1/24

7/9/24

This is the record of Forest Ranger Alan Skudlark. Due to the recent activity and possibility of a potential threat that is being posed towards the staff members assigned to this tower, I intend to find an answer to the current predicament

I've been looking over all the files on this place since the calls came in about the strange happenings and according to the records at the office, there has been an unusually quick turnover rate at this post. What doesn't make sense is that on our end in the rangers office, we continue to get regular check ups and reports that indicate that the watchers were doing fine. Granted, several of them appeared almost robotic and repetitive, but there are only so many ways to say "nothing to report."

I've set up surveillance cameras as well as a few trail cams to try and catch whatever animal desecrated that poor girls remains. The young man we pulled out of here over a month ago still has yet to give a full debriefing. He just kept going on and on about the "Tall Camper." I decided to go off of that and started to do a deep dive of the area. I didn't think I was going to have to do that for the middle of nowhere, but here we are. And was I surprised at what I found.

I discovered that there is a bit of a local urban legend in the area. It goes by a few names, the former rangers and more weathered firewatch crews refer to it as this "Tall Camper." Some of the local tribes called it something else. They said it wasn't a wendigo or a skin walker, those seem to be the most prevalent on the internet today, but instead they called it the visitor from the world below. When I asked or tried to pry some more information, the lines either went silent or what I was told was absurd. One tribesman told me to leave it alone. He called it the "Yahiah." I couldn't find a translation for what it meant, but instead of telling me what it meant, he said "If you are here, it is there."

Another person I ran into also referred to it by that name as well. An old white guy named Carl put it pretty simple. "The sumbitch is tall as shit, and not worth messin' with. If you see the word 'YAHIAH' on anything, best be certain that you should be the one fucking off from that point."

Another claimed he saw it bring down an elk with a single swat of its massive hands. They went on to mention that the natives had known about it long before. However, when I looked it up, there didn't seem to be much on the local tribes or their beliefs, but the comment concerning the odd name from the locals made sense now.

The one that stood out and was willing to give me a lead actually called me. I guess word got around that someone was asking questions, because many that I tried to call went straight to voicemail, families claimed that the people went missing or had been dead for years. However, this guy somehow got my number and what he told me was insane. I'll attach the transcript below.

TRANSCRIPT TEXT CONVERSATION that took place on 7/6/24.

Conversation participants: Alan Skudlark (A.S.) and Anonymous Number (A.N.)

A.S.: HELLO?

A.N.: I understand what you are doing, but I don't agree with it.

A.S.: Who is this?

A.N.: I'm someone who survived what you are looking for.

A.S.: And who am I looking for?

A.N.: It's not a who, it's a what! If you can even call it that. My advice is that you stay away from that place. They'll just make you go missing like the others. They know it's there. They've always known. It just got easier to hide once things went all technological with computers and files.

Things that are easy to change the narrative in. Make others think what going on isn't what's really going on.

A.S.: ...and what would that be?

A.N.: THAT WE WERE FUCKING FOOD! They were feeding us to it. Tower 4 is just a goddamn dog dish. But ya see, I outsmarted them, I figured it out! They try to gaslight you, make you think you are crazy, then they make jokes to try and help you cope. Then when you are delirious and have no clue what's going on, they send you to the beast. They want to appease it. They want to keep it away from the more populated areas. No one cares about a family or two going missing on a camping trip, it's just chalked up to a sad case of people getting turned around in the forest. Shit happens. When that wasn't enough and everyone avoided the area, they sent us in. Once the thing started increasing its hunting grounds, they saw us as the sacrificial lambs.

A.S.: How did you survive?

A.N.: It might not die, but it can still feel pain and at the end of the day, It's an animal. I planted anything I could as an irritant and made the fence a nightmare. Whenever I had to leave, I kept that rifle with me and if I ignored it it left me alone. But the moment I looked at it or paid it any mind, it would turn its sights on me and I had to hope I could find someplace to hide or get back to the tower before it decided to warp reality.

A.S.: Warp reality?

A.N.: You have no clue the things it will show you. It made me see my son... my son! My son had been dead for a year, but there he was, standing outside the fence using the thorns to slit his wrists and tear his skin off. It showed me my wife cheating on me with some faceless man and chasing me through the forest like some two headed, mid fuck centaur. Her moans screeched like a shrinking bell!

A.S.: ...

A.N.: ...(crying)... Please, don't go out there. I shot at it one night. I know I hit it, but the bullet struck the post next to my head. If I can't convince you, at least read the books. Not the bullshit that was sent to your corrupt office, the hard copies in the tower itself. Those are the truth!

A.S.: Wait, don't...

The transcript was ended due to the anonymous caller hanging up.

Note 2

I think going forward, I will be transcribing the important information that is in these log books. I invested in a decent portable solar generator and wrote down the disturbing, yet creepy, rules. They seem pretty simple. Of course they are from the ramblings of a madman. Here they are for anyone reading this.

1. Do not look at whatever this thing is.
2. Be wary of voices and/or people that you see.
3. Do not attack it.

Seems simple enough, and as crazy as I sound, I think I'll trust the deranged ramblings of a mentally destroyed mystery man. Given the evidence at hand, I think it is in my best interest to trust that crazy at the moment. Even if it is insane. At least if I write down the proper clues and rules, then we can train or save future fire watchers. At least until we can kill it.

7/10/24

This is Alan Skudlark reporting on my first day at Tower 4. The clean up team has already collected most of Brittani's belongings. Her parents were told they could collect them after the investigation.

They were understandably upset at this, but the supernatural seems to be the main thought of the locals, some of the medical experts and detectives seem determined to say that there is a possible killer on the loose. However, the skeptic in me is still thinking it was just an unfortunate violent bear attack and nothing else.

Do I think the idea that there is some psychopath out here killing people? Yeah, there is a slim, non-zero chance, but with seeing what happened to that girl–not to mention how traumatized that kid was. I have only ever seen that kind of reaction from wild animal attacks.

I think I'm gonna settle in and organize my stuff. Maybe I'll look for those log books, if they even exist. I'll let ya know if I find anything.

7/11/24

My search last night was not in vain. I found the boxes of old files and log books that the anonymous caller mentioned. Maybe there was some truth to his words? It looks like someone had already curated them from 1911 to at least the mid 70s. The most recent entries seem to have jumped to this year. Mr. Brunstein must have found it. I can't believe that the investigators never checked these, or maybe they did and just ignored it. If what the mystery caller said is true, it wouldn't shock me.

Note 2

There was no better place to start than with the first file that mentions seeing this thing. I pulled out the oldest file and it was from Gilbert Fulton, he was one of the first tower watch guys in the beginning.

The excerpt that was of interest was from 8/13/ 1911. The tail end of this man's service.

"Gilbert Fulton, day 135 of my watch. It has been an interesting summer. We haven't had too many people being disturbances, but I have been seeing someone wandering the woods, and the other towers have mentioned seeing the same odd camper.

At first, I thought it was some transient, maybe a hobo? Given how he's been wandering around, he might just be a homeless person. The nearest train track is a two day ride from here by horse. Even further to the station.

I didn't pay them no mind up till this point, but the fellow appears to be causing an issue with my lady friend in the neighboring tower to the west. She claims that this transient appears to be watching her from a cliff. She even said that she saw them standing in her fenceline. Not hiding, but just standing there like one of them retarded fellas from the state.

I might take a meander tonight. See if I can find our unwanted guest's campsite. Don't need some pervert making things difficult for Annie, can't say I blame him though, from what I hear, she is pretty easy on the eyes."

This wasn't the final entry into the log for that year. However, the subsequent entries all appeared to be generic and the final entry was a simple "another one for the books."

I'm going to continue researching this. Maybe this is some kind of long thought extinct animal? Or proof we were all wrong and the Native Americans had it right. Who knows, but it's a lead.

7/12/24

I checked the trail cams today, but nothing other than a lone coyote and a few curious racoons. I checked in with the other towers, but none reported anything unusual. Angela appears to be in good spirits considering her last coworker was just torn apart and the one before that went nuts. Her excuse when questioned was that the isolation does strange things to people out here. I wasn't present for that, but I was assured by my supervisors that she had nothing to do with the murder. Not to mention that, supposedly, at the estimated time of the attack, she was with one of the other watchers at a supply drop.

I reviewed the footage from last night and as expected, it came up short for anything exciting as well. I decided to just go in chronological order with the log books last night while trying to make myself tired. Doesn't make any sense to not try and learn all I can with all the down time.

The next written mentions of this thing took place a few years later. Abraham Jones left a short note on 5/25/1917 as well as a full report from 6/22/1917.

"It is not the best way to find out about our country going to war, but I just heard along the wire that we are entering the conflict on the other side of the world.

Not like I could do anything about it, might get drafted. Who knows though. Maybe I'll get lucky and just be stuck out here instead. At least I'll be safe enough out here for a few months.

Anna, in tower 3, contacted me today. She said that she saw something straight out of the traveling freakshow. She told me that she saw what looked like two female campers standing far off through the trees in their birthday suits holding hands. She said that they were smiling, but the longer she stayed there, the more things didn't seem right. She said the smiles looked painted on and their eyes were covered by dirty hair. And here's the even nuttier part, she claims that when she really looked, it became clear that the hands weren't clasped together, but the arms themselves appeared to be attached at the wrist.

It must have been a translation error, because what she was saying made no sense. I'll have to report that someone might be tapping our clicker lines as a joke."

What followed the note, was an "official" confirmation that someone had spliced into the line. That was the story they stuck to, but the tower operators weren't the ones to confirm that.

6/22/1917 was the second mention of this thing. This was his first personal interaction with the creature. However, it appears to have been cut off at some point. It was also his last long entry.

"I made it into one of the caves. I don't know what was wrong with that camper, but something wasn't right with them, and they were so tall. I didn't realize how far they were away until I was too close for it to be safe.

I thought they were lost and kept calling to them. The whole time they were just staring at me like I was some imaginary critter coming out of the wilderness to greet them. I thought they might have been on that wacky tobacky, but the closer I got, just... something seemed to be off about them.

Their limbs seemed to be too long for their body, the stance they had was as if at complete ease and absolutely still. I think that was the first thing that made me feel uneasy. The whole time I was walking through the overgrowth, it didn't move so much as an inch. The closer I got caused more details to sharpen.

It almost looked like a sculpture standing there. Like one of those realism artist types put one of their wastes-of-time out here. Its size though, when I got closer, would have made that impossible. We were in the middle of nowhere and this thing looked like it weighed a ton.

I couldn't help but admire it for what it was, though. Its skin looked to have been some sort of thin leather stretched so tight against its body that in some areas it already started to tear, its clothing seemed to be part of its body, not stitched on, but as if its skin was trying to imitate the shape and colors. Like a chameleon, made of human flesh. The hat that I thought it was wearing was sealed to the top of its head like a mushroom cap. Its wrinkled face had splotches of color roughly where its eyes, mouth and nose should be. It looked more like someone tried to mimic a face on lumpy flesh using shadows.

Its towering form appeared to be in a friendly posture, almost as if it was leaned back to wave. The elongated limbs distorted the figure and instead of appearing friendly, it looked like it was posturing to show its dominance. Like you would picture Dracula standing at the top of a staircase, only instead of contempt and judgment, it was intimidatingly asking to borrow some sugar at your front door.

I was so caught up staring at this strange avatar of the woods, that I didn't even notice that while I was looking at it, its head had tilted down and was, by my approximation, now peering down at me.

It was a subtle movement, but it was enough to let me know that whatever this beast was, it was alive. As soon as I understood what was going on, I started running. I never ran so fast in my life.

I could see the tower in the distance, but I changed my direction when I saw something standing on the catwalk. Its size was undeniable and it appeared to be watching me. I turned back to see if I was being pursued, but the one I had approached was gone. The thought that it could just vanish and appear like a magic show was mind boggling to me.

I found shelter in this cave and I don't think it saw where I came in. I doubt that it could fit..."

The rest of the entry was torn out from the book. It looked to have been covered in dirt and stone at some point. There was even some water damage. It was clearly weathered more than the other volumes, so I don't think this was found in the filing cabinet.

"Another one for the books" was written at the top of the page that was torn off. Maybe search and rescue found this guy, and this is where the tradition started? Who knows? I'm going to check the cameras and call it a night.

But the thought that there may be more than one thing out here for me to worry about is slightly concerning. Oh god, listen to me. I'm talking like this is all real. This all could be just an elaborate hoax. However, you would have to be a real asshole to be playing a joke on someone right after a tragedy, and to possibly use real missing persons reports too... that's just sick.

Note 1

Something tripped one of the cameras. When I reviewed the images though, it must have been set up wrong because the shots were all washed out. I could see some shadows, but nothing concrete of what caused it. But given what time the picture was taken, lens flair shouldn't have been an issue. The sun would have been behind the unit. Unless something is right up against it? No, it would have been caught on camera long before it could have gotten that close...

Wait... where did the time go? It's already dark out? I guess time really does fly when you are focussed on something important.

7/13/24

It was strange, last night I couldn't sleep so I spent some time trying to enhance that image. Out of curiosity I put it through a few filters. When I got to the negative filter, it showed much more and the form was human – or at the very least some animal on its hind legs. Which in of itself is inherently creepy to picture in my mind. Last thing I wanna see is an elk or deer, running at me like a person. It did answer my question of if there was something that close to the camera.

The figure looked to be holding something in its hands, but the odd part was that whatever it was holding seemed to be what was causing the lens flare. As if the light was emanating from some weird sphere floating above an open book or map.

I'm guessing it was some camper with a laser or something, flashing the lens. However, that is equally as disturbing knowing that there was someone else this far away from civilization and willing to mess with property that isn't their own. It was an uncomfortable notion.

I know that according to the stories, a bullet won't stop this "Tall Camper," but knowing there might be a person like that out here, I'm gonna be sleeping with this gun next to me going forward.

I went for a patrol today trying to find where Jones had escaped to. I must have walked ten miles. I checked every hole in a rock big enough to hide in, but nothing seemed to be making any sense. From the way his note read, the place he went to couldn't have been too far from the tower. I couldn't even locate the one the crew found that kid in.

I eventually had to give up on my search, due to losing light in the day, but I did make a fun discovery when I got back to the tower. I noticed that some of the fence had been damaged. Something had come across my camp and torn down some of the thorn bushes, revealing some damage that had been done to the gate at some point in its long life.

I went to see what was in the shed and discovered that the tools were a little worse for wear, but I found some linemens and wire. I might not be able to grow a bunch of thorn bushes at the moment, but I can add some sharp deterrents for would-be "explorers." It took me a few hours, but repairing the gate was simple enough. Just bending the piece back into the correct shape and shackling it back into place.

I spoke to Angela tonight, she's been putting up a strong front, given the consistent loss of coworkers. The possibility of some deranged killer, or some ancient Native American demon from their equivalent of hell, coming up here for a visit.

She just kept saying that with how long she's been on firewatch, nothing freaks her out. She's met her fair share of people claiming to have seen bigfoot and aliens. Even had a few mentions of finding sculptures in the forest. She didn't see the point in worrying about stuff she didn't believe in. To her, those people were just those that got lost and after a while their brains just played tricks on them. It's just an inconvenient truth of the matter.

I don't remember when she joined, but the stories she shared with me were quite elaborate. She once found a few kids that had been hiking for days covered in dirt and moving as quietly as possible. It was a brother and sister. They had been separated from their parents and when they tried to find them they followed what sounded like their mother and fathers voices calling their names.

They just kept going, and eventually they got to a clearing where she ended up stumbling across them during her morning hike. At first, she shouted for them but they acted very strange. They pretended as if they couldn't hear her. She said that as she got closer, a strange feeling of dread wormed its way up her legs making her feel wobbly. She said it was like her legs were noodles and she felt the urge to shit, like after eating a questionable amount of cheese while being lactose intolerant.

When she got close enough, she could see the two breathing heavily like they were hyperventilating. She gently tried to put a hand on the older sister's shoulder to let them know they were safe, but they just screamed, not looking at her, and took off running back into the forest.

She eventually caught up with them, but all she got out of them was, "It wasn't mom!" It was an odd situation to explain to the rangers, but as far as she was aware, those kids were reunited with their parents and their psychosis was due to not having eaten and exposure for a few days. She would have been more worried if they hadn't been delusional.

I asked her, "Why?" And she goes on to say "Because if you are a couple of kids, out here and having just survived something traumatic, if you aren't seeing and hearing weird shit, you are a certified psychopath. Next thing ya know, we see them on one of those crime shows saying they were found running some sort of incest cult that eats babies while stomping bags of kittens and puppies that may or may not be associated with your rank and or who you marry in the family."

I told her that seemed oddly specific, but she brushed it off saying, "I've seen it a hundred times. Those little nutjobs heard the Donner party and grabbed those stupid birthday cone hats with the rubber thingy and a fork. They knew what was gonna happen and they would show up ready to barbecue a bitch."

I had no clue how to argue that logic, but it did give me a bit of levity to break up my rising anxiety. It was a well needed reprieve. I know I'm out here to search for answers, but it's only two weeks into July. I still have another month and a half until I'm picked up. Even though I want my answers, I gotta remember to stay grounded.

I think I'm gonna go do a sweep of the area before bed. I haven't received any notifications of cameras going off, or any movement for that matter. I think I'll go through a few more of those logs. That should help pass the time.

7/14/24

I think I saw it today while I was checking the cameras. I know I should be terrified. I guess to a degree I am, but it was kind of exhilarating.

I went to the east and rounded an old ancient tree trunk that must have been cut down decades ago. It was kind of a landmark. For the locals. I don't know how true their stories are, but they say that way back when the town was founded, the settlers cut it down to build the first building. They forced the native tribes out, and slaughtered those that fought back. All for some gold.

It wasn't long after the establishment of the little boomtown that stories of monstrous creatures lurked in the forests. There were those that were easily debunked as grizzly bears, but they didn't know what they were back then. However, the few stories that remained throughout the years have been about those that traveled further west.

I came across an elder from one of the remaining tribes in the area during my initial investigation in the nearest town, who told me that in the western forest, there is a demon from the world below. That the invasion of the white man across these lands disturbed the balance. The native peoples suffering and the destruction of the sacred lands the ancients had bartered for their safety was being destroyed.

What came from below was a protector of sorts. You could say that the elder gods of the people had grown quite fond of the lands and weren't too happy that someone came and destroyed their piece of the pie. What followed were tales so terrible that it made a ghost town out of the place.

The elder went on to tell me that the clearings are where the processing of the ore was done. That the protector scorched the earth in a shining light and when it was done, all that remained was an open, desolate field. As it walked away, the grass grew from the ash. It was as if with a wave of one hand it could take away life, and with the other, it forced life to come from death.

She smiled at me and told me not to come here. That the protector has grown tired of all trespassers on the land, that although it was understanding, it no longer tolerated any transgressions.

As the memory of that conversation left my thoughts, I had made my way around the massive trunk to face the west and I saw something hidden in the blind of the trees. A moment later, it was gone in a rush of wind.

I turned away and remembered the rules. Don't acknowledge it.

I decided to come back here and make my daily log after checking the cameras. I think the rest of the day will be just reading. I'll make a note if I find anything interesting.

7/16/24

I was so caught up in reading I lost track of time. I don't even remember seeing the sun go down or come back up. I did however find one doozy of a story written in a log from the 50s. The few other mentions and entries up until that point were pretty consistent with what I've experienced. Glimpses from the side or off in the distance. Something obscures it. Yet this entry was a trip.

7/4/54

This place can go straight to whatever hell it came from. Those poor kids, I swear I didn't kill them, but what purpose could that creature even serve in your grand plan, Lord?

All it was, was a couple of fireworks. Antonia called it in over the squawk box, but I could see them from my tower clear as day. I spent three hours in the dark, hiking through that bramble patch of weeds, using the darn flashes like I was looking for baby jesus.

I swear on my life, I wasn't going to do anything with that young girl. We were in the tent, but that didn't mean we weren't doing anything inappropriate. I followed procedure, all I did was scare them a little. Not like I'm a cop, I ain't allowed to arrest nobody. So I made due.

I thought it was done. I took their stash and scared them a bit, but when I was done doin' that I was done. When I came back this morning... the whole campsite was destroyed. There wasn't any blood, or bodies, but the whole lot of them were simply gone. Poof!

I searched the woods as far as I could, but I couldn't find any tracks leading out. I thought maybe they left their trash, but there were still tents set up, torn to shreds some of them, but up nonetheless. Their bonfire was ice cold, as if not having been lit for hours.

I heard screams and I ran, I feared there was a bear attacking one of the kids. I chased the terrified cries for help. I don't know for how long, but I followed all the same. I might not have been able to fight a bear, but I could at least draw its attention. Maybe scare it by showing there were more of us than of it.

I remember being told to avoid the western portion of the forest, but I thought they were just ghost stories to scare the less attuned to the wilderness away. We got enough city folk going missing, no sense in more coming to join the roster.

The further I went, the forest became darker as the sun set.. After what must have been hours, I finally saw someone walking in the distance. I shouted and waved, but she kept walking. The closer I got, the more it became clear she seemed to be moving in a general direction. Like she was in some catatonic state.

She was dragging a blanket behind her. Whenever it snagged a branch or on a rock. She would stumble until it pulled free. When I caught up to her, she tried to walk through me, until I was able to get her to focus on my eyes. She screamed in my face, as if I was some monster, before collapsing into my arms. It was far too late to be heading back to the tower. There was just no way we could even attempt the trek at night out here.

Instead, I ended up making camp. I fashioned the tattered blanket into a tent and struggled to try and start a fire. With each strike of my matches, there was a slight spark of light. This must have been what set the girl off, because as soon as one of the matches took a flame, she again lost control and attacked me. She shoved me to the ground and stomped out the tiny whiff of light.

At first I thought she was just crazy, but when she collapsed in tears, I figured best not to yell at her. Maybe whatever happened the night before had to do with fire? I decided to help her to the tent and gave her some water.

Between the sniffles and gentle sobs, we must have fallen asleep, because the next thing I knew, I felt my arm being squeezed and I woke up to a hand across my mouth.

I did my best to stay calm as I looked into the scared eyes of the young woman. Even in the low light I could hear the quiet "shush" that she mouthed to me. The world was silent and I felt my heart race as I followed the girl's eyes towards the foot of our gerry-rigged tent, only to see a massive shadow of a head just inside of the threshold. The neck was craned at an unnatural angle right above our feet.

I couldn't see any features, but I felt its gaze. I felt another squeeze on my arm. I had to force myself to look away as I heard a scream come from the girl's direction. I could still feel her deathgrip, but when I turned to face her, she was gone. The blanket wall wasn't moving. It wasn't as if she was pulled from under it. She was just gone! The only thing I could hear was the almost vibrating scream as it echoed until that too suddenly ended. Stolen from the air like a bird snatching a worm.

I slowly turned back to look at the still stationary face. After a few moments, it looked like it began to pull itself out of the draped cloth while simultaneously getting closer to me before it too vanished and bled into the darkness.

I stayed awake the rest of the night, staring off into the black until the gentle light of the morning lit up where we were. I could see the sun rising in the east, but there were no trees blocking my view. I remembered we were surrounded by them last night, but now I wasn't even in the same place as then.

There was a weak tapping sound on metal and I scrambled out from the blanket and I found myself at the base of my tower.

Now I'm here, writing this, and the utter absence of sound is terrifying me.

"Another one for the books"

Note 2

That was the final entry for that season. The final report was from the rangers that found him in the fall. His body had been ceremoniously cut all the way to the bone and flayed open. The muscle and skin, nailed to the trees, his skeletal remains were made into an effigy under the rotted warning.

That was kind of an intense story for me. I think I'm gonna start a project tomorrow. Maybe I'll make the shed into my little report den and I can track where this thing is staying? Or at least figure out where each of these deaths took place.

7/19/24

Ok, ok, I know it's been a few days again, but I've full on, swan dived into this rabbit hole of a story here. What I have been up to though is I started piecing things together. If what the elder told me was true then that would mean that the visions these people were seeing, that I was seeing, weren't just some hysteria that all of us that work these towers are suffering from.

I spent more time going through the logs and I missed one from the 40s. When I saw the date I thought it was a joke... or like karma.

8/7/1946

I can't believe they did it... I get that they destroyed our ships, but even I think that the destruction of two cities... all those innocent people? Gone in a flash. That was too far.

The start of the atomic age has begun. I heard from Aretha this morning. It was too early for the reports of casualties, but I wonder how many were just brainwashed civilians.

I could understand if we had bombed the Germans, but this... I need to go for a walk.. Maybe that will help clear my head. Maybe a smoke or two can ease my conscience.

Note 2

I think I killed it, or at least have it buried under enough rubble that it will never see the light of day again. I found a cave to the west and it followed me in. I heard my brother's voice in the woods. How could it sound like him? He's half a world away. He was drafted into the war effort. What the hell is happening?

It showed me... things, horrible things. Faceless soldiers marching. Golems of flesh that looked like women and children forced into ovens! The trees warped into the shapes like clay being molded and brought to life.

The forest flashed and all was hell. A single figure strode to the center of it. Its clasped hands held at its chest, one hand on top of the other. Its face unlike the others had eyes, black as the depths of the ocean, a single slit, crossed where its mouth should be at an angle. Like a knife had been slashed from its ear to the opposite side of its chin.

I fell back and frantically scuttled away to put as much distancebetween us as it tilted its darkened eyes in my direction. A sadness in them made me stop my escape, even if for a moment, until the rest of its body followed. Each step it took, the now charred remains, crumbled and washed away in the wind.

My body moved as if trapped in sand. I could feel its presence closing, I did not know what other horrors it wished to show me, but it was clear this avatar of wrath incarnate was going to take its hatred out on me. I ran for the old mine.The creature was far too large to fit in its narrow halls and I knew there was an exit I could escape through.

I ran until my chest burned and my lungs stung as if I had just smoked a pack of cigarettes. All the while I could see but not hear the beast approach. Its sickly taught skin twitching with anticipation.

I jumped into the mine entrance, scrambled to my feet and took a breath of relief, only for it to be stripped from me with the sound of the very stone around me beginning to crack. I looked back to the entrance and the creature was bent down in a way that made it look like it didn't have a spine. Its upper body twisted like a snake as it followed me.

I had been exploring this mine for a few weeks now, so I had a pretty good grip of where I could go. I descended into one of the tunnels, knowing what was down here.

I snatched an old lantern I had used in my adventures down here, and lit it. The monster was now defying gravity by walking down the wall. Its onyx eyes reflected the flame. The shadows of its face made it look like a dance of different emotions.

I ran down the corridor, grabbed a sack off the ground and found the ladder out. Each rung felt like a step to freedom. When I made it to the top, I waited until I saw its shadow and I tossed the bag down. When it hit, several sticks flew in all directions.

I turned to see the light from my exit point. It was only sixty feet away. I tossed the lantern and mustered what strength I had left and started to sprint. I made it three steps before I heard the glass shatter and the metal smack off the rock. A second later, the ground shook as a concussive heatwave licked at my back. The blast blew out my eardrums, but I made it out of there. I don't know how long dynomite lasts, but I'm glad it still went boom.

I still can't hear, even as I write this, but the tunnel collapsed behind me. I'm going to have a smoke and...

The entry ended there. And like the others, it ended with the rangers making their entry upon finding the remains. Mr. Tim Lorrain, was later found four miles from the tower. His scalp had been torn off and a large animal jaw was used like a meat hook driven deep into his chest and he was hung from a tree growing out of a cliff face, four hundred feet straight up. No matter how you math it, there is no way any man was going to carry an almost two hundred pound man up a sheer wall, plus equipment, and then climb out without leaving a single shred of evidence.

Date of death, though, didn't match the entry. But like the others it still ended with "Another one for the books."

I later added the date to the board. So far, from what I can tell, is that this thing is bulletproof, fireproof, and explosion proof. It seems to come out only when someone goes to the western side of the territory. Something in that territory also appears to affect time.

The age of it is over a hundred and fifty years old. I only have a few more of these logs left in the basket. That means that if these are all that I have, what happened to the rest of them? Did the others just not report anything? Or did they figure out how to survive? What is it that they did?

In the 60s, there was another war based mention of the creature. The watcher was a bit off. He was a vet that was sent home. From what I've read, I don't think it was for a good reason, but a necessary one.

5/14/61

I don't know what yall want me to write in this, but I do want to say thank you for letting me work for you. I... I didn't get a warm welcome home and not that I deserve it, but still, the fact you were willing to give me a home and a job in my time of need, I thank you.

My name is Frank Delong, this is my first entry since finding this book here. Not much to report. They said the last fella just up and went god knows where. Said that he might have left with one of those communes or whatever those hippies call them. Spent the worst part of the last five years of my life in the shit, fighting those commie little fucks, but here we are back in America and those pansy-ass kids that can't see the bigger picture are trying to live like the enemy. Thinking some free love bullshit and giving each other massages while doing drugs is a way to survive. They don't know a damn thing about survival.

Anyways, you told me to keep an eye out for any of them. There have been reports that the idiots have set up shop out here of all places. I guess it's not the worst idea I've seen or heard of. Plenty of food to forage and water to drink.

5/24/61

I haven't had a good night's sleep in so long. Yet out here, it's as if the screams are finally silent for a change. I remember the first few nights upon my return home... I couldn't even be in a dark room without seeing them.

Glossed over eyes from the dark. The shadows standing around me as I lay in bed. Their words muttered in a language I never learned to speak. I begged for their forgiveness, for what my squad did. I tried to stop them! However, in the end, I either had to help, or join the people in that unmarked pit.

Maybe it's something to do with the immersion here. It's no jungle, but the redwoods and pines that surround me right now have made it more... tolerable. Looking at this sunrise right now, sure I've seen it on a more violent horizon in the past, but maybe this is how I start to heal.

5/29/61

Amber from tower 3 radioed me today. She told me that a few campers saw what looked like a little tent city about four miles west of my tower. She said that the area is pretty dense, and that I should bring the rifle from the storage locker. It's not that she is scared that a couple of tree huggers could get the drop on me, but she told me there have been reports of a strange animal.

I laughed at her concern because where I was stationed, the bigger animals weren't nearly as terrifying as the smaller bugs. I'm not saying I can take a bear in a fist fight, but I played dead as a Vietcong conscript was bayonetting my dead comrade right next to me. I think I can handle doing that with an animal. If worse comes to worse, I could always do what my commander told us, "I don't care what you have to do, shit your pants if need be or die! You do not wanna be sent to the Hanoi Hilton!".

8/13/61

WHAT THE FUCK HAVE I DONE!? All of them dead. THEY ARE ALL DEAD! Oh god, they took me in, they showed me a love that I had never felt and my thanks to them for that was... I... I can't go back. I can't unbury those people! If I'm gonna be arrested though, I at least want to have my side written down.

I went to the location that Amber told me about. After a half day of hiking and circumventing dangerous terrain, I found the area that the campers reported. It wasn't hard to find from there. The smell of weed and the sound of drums were a dead giveaway.

I snuck up on the campsite. It wasn't hard, they were so stoned that even if I had just walked in and sat with them, I doubt they would have even noticed. But the scary part happened when I looked west of the commune and I saw... something... looking at me.

I shook the vision away, but in doing so I found myself back in the rice paddies. It looked familiar, but I couldn't place it yet. I crawled through the mud and took cover beside a small shed. Closing my eyes, I took a deep breath and prepared myself, but when I looked around the corner, I found that I was simply looking at the hippies.

There were fifteen or so of them. They were just relaxing and were enjoying the forest. They had no clue what was out here, but to them it was just nature. To me, I was watching them like a predator eyeing its next tasty meal.

I stood up and found myself back in Vietnam. I raised my rifle and began my approach. Each step I took, the sky grew darker. Storm clouds rolled in fast. I was maybe twelve yards from the Cong, they were oblivious to my approach. I took aim at one of the units in the group.

I flicked the safety on the rifle and placed my finger on the trigger. The tiny sound attracted their attention and the one I had trained in my sights turned to face me. She was a young girl who couldn't have been more than eighteen or nineteen. I recognized her and in the blink of an eye, I was back in the forest. A blank expression.Ginger girl sitting with her eyes wide open and her pupils blown out from whatever she was tripping on was now looking back at me.

I looked at the rest of the now silent unmoving group, all of them with the same glazed look. As if there, but not really there at the same time. For all I knew, they saw me as an elephant only man sized wearing a clown costume, because out of nowhere, they opened their mouths and I heard laughing. But the expressions on their faces didn't match the sound.

They didn't move, and I don't remember approaching, but I found myself in the center of their gathering. The redhead I had been pointing my gun at was stood in front of me and all of a sudden I felt myself being embraced.

It wasn't as if I was being attacked, but it was the group hugging me and a wave of calming love washed over me. I knew the feeling from back when my ex-wife and kids would run up and meet me at the door. I didn't want to go to war! But when I got back… "They just couldn't handle who I was now," was their main excuse, but she never listened to me. My former squadmates turned me into a scapegoat and blamed the slaughter THEY did on me. They told my wife that I raped the women, that I skewered a baby on a broom handle and beat the mother to death. They told the doctors I was not mentally sound anymore to serve my country, but when push came to shove, those monsters couldn't take accountability for their actions and blamed it all on me. What they forced me to engage in was a war crime!

Now I am here, standing in the center of something I haven't felt in months and I didn't know how starved I was for it. I found myself relaxing and the warped reality of the memory and the now, became clear.

I was with them for weeks, I learned their way of life. It was beautiful. The joy and acceptance. They understood I was hurt and that I needed to learn how to let go. We had no names, we never spoke of them, we were all one.

It felt as if months had gone by. I was the happiest I had ever been… until the storm came. We had all shared a pot of mushroom tea. I had been opening my mind with them in this way for several *weeks now. This wasn't something new, but what happened next once the storm started, I don't know.*

I remember the rain, the cool sprinkles hitting my skin and dampening my clothes as the mushrooms began to kick in. It felt amazing. It tickled slightly, but in a good way, and the trails of the water looked like rivers against my arms and hands. The sounds of the forest were drowned out by the barrage of excess moisture bouncing off the needles. The smell of wet pine mixed with whatever was composting into the earth filled my nostrils and I could see the fabric of space vibrate with the trillions of impacts all around us.

I followed the trails and found their source. They lead in an arc across the sky. It wasn't so much that it was falling, but more, being thrown or launched like artillery. My eyes traced it and I saw it funneling down until I saw the source. The stranger from before when I first got here was there with one of its odd shaped hands held out as if offering the little tornado of wetness to me.

Next thing I knew I was being held down on a rat infested mattress. The shadows stood around me again with the largest holding my arms and legs, all of their lifeless slanted eyes filled with black hatred. Their tattered clothes were stained brown with dried blood. The bodies seemed to shift in and out of existence.

I knew the danger I was in and I had to escape. I did what any soldier would have done, I fought. I fought like a rabid animal. Hit after hit, I tore through the contacts and dragged their wicked bodies into the fields.

I killed my way through the small platoon, their bodies crumbling to the ground like sacks of rotten tomatoes. The last one, a young Vietnamese girl, struggled to catch her breath. I had surprised her and when she tried to stab me, I dodged the knife and repeatedly punched her in the throat.

I knelt down beside her, covering her nose and mouth. Her eyes widened as she knew what was happening. You never forget how it feels to end someone's life like that. The power, the control... the regret.

I looked up to the sky as the rain stopped and I felt the struggling body beneath me finally stop squirming. Looking to the west, I saw the being closing its hand into a fist before it held its hands out, mimicking like it was holding a bowl or a book.

I looked around me again and I was back in the camp. When I turned my attention down to the ground though I fell back as I saw the redheaded girl's lifeless bloodshot eyes staring up at me. I saw the others and the realization hit me of what happened. I could hear their mumbled moans of anguish as if they were still alive, just unmoving. Like looking at a pile of dead fish on a boat deck.

I didn't know what else to do, but as I write this I know it was wrong of me, but I found a shovel and started to dig. I was going to hide this mistake like I did a year ago. But now I feel so much guilt. I could still hear their screams even through four feet of dirt.

I can't be here anymore. The extraction team will be here in a few weeks. I can't be here when they get here or else I'm going to be put in front of the firing squad.

9/1/61

Search and rescue entry. Upon arrival we discovered the confession written in this log book. We do not know where Frank Delong is, but with the size of this place he could be anywhere. We contacted tower 3, but she has no recollection of ever telling Frank about any campers or the hippies for that matter.

Note 1

Search and rescue entry. A sister search party has discovered a mass grave four miles west of Tower 4. According to them, it appears that the victims weren't all dead when initially buried. The sick bastard buried some of them alive.

"ANOTHER ONE FOR THE BOOKS."

7/19/24

I did what I could to research these incidents, but nothing showed up other than a missing persons report and a warrant for his arrest. I don't know if Mr. Delong killed those campers, but from the evidence at hand... I'm just glad that since it was so long ago, he surely is dead by now.

Note 2

Checked the camera, nothing to report.

8/1/24

I don't know how else to say this... but... I think the only way for me to put this and keep it as the hundred percent truth, I need to just staple the next few pages to this log. They were much longer and far more complete than the others. But the messed up part is how did he know? How did he survive? Will I survive?

6/4/76

Welcome and salutations to those of this great country. Founded on the love of Christian values and a gun. Sure we may have had to pull out of a war, but here we are, living to pray another day.

I figured it would be best to commemorate such a beautiful day with a blessing. Remembering the day that our forefathers fought and brought this bleak savage infested land into the light of the new age. Uplifting the lawless lands into the modern day and fighting off an oppressive ruler. HAPPY BICENTENNIAL!

Note 1

I saw someone hiking today. A tall fella. It looked like he was reading a book. When I brought it up to Amara over the horn, she told me to not bother them, but it has been a few months since I've seen anyone else, let alone talked face to face. If my missionary work has taught me anything, a lone soul in the woods is wandering away from the truth of life, and I am just the stranger to help lead him on the path to salvation.

I'm off to convert another brother into the wonderful truth of the good and joyous lord. I shall return with another note when the lost sheep has been brought to the light.

Note 2

Well... not all converts are willing, but with a more... humbled appearance. I believe I have learned an important lesson. That demons roam these woods. That man I saw was a heathen of the pagan gods. His sin cooked into his savage red skin.

I know how our country was founded and what happened to their people, but if they had simply accepted the almighty's divine embrace instead of choosing to continue on with their foolish beliefs, maybe we wouldn't have had to punish them for their sins. However, this gentleman had clearly felt hellfire.

His face was scarred and ghoulish in its appearance that I've only seen once before. How he had navigated these woods, I don't know. But he was clearly a severe burn victim. His eyes were gone and his stride was gangly. Even the scar tissue that was his skin seemed only wrapped around tumorous bones.

Our ancestors came to this land to practice in peace. We didn't need the annoyance of temptation to unfounded gods. There is only one God and I'll be damned if some mongoloid of an "elder" has an appearance like that to take my true faith away.

I don't know what happened after he turned away. I woke up soaking in the cool waters of the spring. My body was covered in bruises and every movement felt like I had just been through a battle.

I got dressed and by the time I got back here, my skin was on fire. I might have to go back to that stream. Hopefully the good Lord will see fit to lend me a healing hand.

6/5/76

Where in the blue blazes did he find a horse? When I got back from another soaking session to purge my body of whatever was causing this burning rash, I looked off my balcony, and that giant of a man was sitting on a pale horse. I don't remember seeing any sign of one the other day,. And I don't know if it was the distance, but it didn't look like he had legs, or if he did, they looked fused, melted even, to the emaciated creature.

In the moment that I saw him, a gust of wind came and his chest puffed out like a sail. The living corpse opened its mouth and I heard what I guess was some kind of warcry, but its mouth seemed stretched further than what would be natural and didn't seem to move. In fact, the whole time they were there they didn't so much as snort or breathe. After an uncomfortable amount of time, they rode off into the trees.

I don't know to what end, but I reported it to Amara. She actually got mad that I didn't listen, but I don't need to listen to her. I only do as she asks as a courtesy because she's technically my boss out here and has so many years of experience. This place needs a real man, like myself, to tame the wilds. Now, I think I'll head back to the stream. Maybe that will help temper the edge on this issue. The burn is making me see things I think.

Note 1

He came back! I woke up to some kind of howl in the night. Everything was dead silent. Even the usually incessant mosquitos weren't making any noise.

When I went to the window, I saw the horse standing at the gate. I turned the spotlight on it and it looked up to me, its eye almost looked like it was just painted on skin. Once it noticed I was watching, it began to viciously grind its face against the chainlink. Its flesh tore like cheese going through a grater. All the while, filling the void of silence with its cries.

I don't know what devilry this was, but the whines became more like scared women and children screaming. I grabbed the rifle, and looked down through the scope, only to see a pile of chunky flesh and bone on my side of the fence, the hamburger meat of the animal's remaining part of its head turned and another painted on eye looked up to me.

I don't know what came over me, but I felt a sense of doom deep in my chest as the bloodied tongue draped out of its mouth overtop what was left of its lower jaw and licked across the remaining teeth of the upper jaw. An otherworldly force hit me and I felt a sharp pain in my heart.

I must have passed out because I woke up on the floor beside my bed. I will admit that it wasn't one of my prouder positions, but I haven't drank anything since last night while I was soaking.

I rushed to the window and looked where the disturbing sight should have been. It was pitch black and the sounds of the night were back. I ran outside to the flood lamp and lit up the area again, and saw that there was still something where the horse's face shreds had piled.

Note 2

It was bones. Random, burnt animal bones. On top of it was a dream catcher made of skin and hair. I don't know if it was animal hide, but I swear I saw part of a tattoo on one of the strips.

I have to wait to radio Amara in the morning. I'm sure she's gonna say some snarky feminist "I told you so" type crap, but I need her to know that someone is actively harassing me. Hope she can get off her high horse long enough to listen to reason.

7/1/76

This blasted burning sensation hasn't gone away! I've been soaking in that cold water several times a day, but all I get is a moment's reprieve. And every night that bastard shows up now. I put up crucifixes, but each one seems to burn my hands more than the last. Is this a test? Is the lord testing me as he did Job?

7/23/76

It knows what I did... It showed me the memory of that day. They weren't people, they were just the dirty non believers lying to my face so they could get a fucking apple or whatever other rotted food we were sent to give them to barter their faith.

Through their dirty false smiles they would beg, why shouldn't I have taken my due from them. I was their salvation. The least they could do was satisfy me.

8/10/76

I know what I did was wrong, but if God didn't want it to be a part of his plan, he would have stopped me, right? He even stood by as his own son was hammered to the cross. He allowed good men and women to be slaughtered for the greater good.

This is a test of my measure. I have been chosen to bare his word into these savage lands of sexual deviants and drug powered politicians. I AM THE CHOSEN!

This burning is to remind me that all ascension is brought about through sacrificing oneself, and giving up your earthly needs of comfort. To cast aside the poison of comfort. I will be a saint amongst men. I will be one of his disciples.

8/31/76

IF I TAKE OFF MY SKIN IT CAN'T HURT ME! I REMOVED ONE OF MY EYES ALREADY. I SEE NOW THAT I WAS WRONG, THE YAHIAH IS THE TRUE GOD! IT WANTS PENANCE, I'LL GIVE IT ALL!

9/1/76

Ranger Torez, final report. We found a lot of blood, but no sign of a body. We discovered a drying rack made of wood and tied together with what looks like human hair. On the rack we found crudely cut strips of desiccated meat. I don't know what happened here, but with the amount of blood we found on the ground out here, I'd be surprised if the watcher is still alive. Man, what is it about this place attracting crazies?

"Another one for the books."

8/17/24

Those were the last logs in the book for that year. In fact, that was the last entry, before I found the book for this year. Something about them doesn't make sense and I"m sure you will pick up on what I mean.

When I was dropped in, I brought my own log book for records keeping, but this is a world of information. That even I have no clue about, and trust me, it is best that I put the last two entries in, in their entirety for them to make sense by the end of it. Believe me.

4/1/24

I'm not gonna lie, these stairs SUCK!!! They didn't tell me how tall this tower was, just the pay. So, well, here I am. Day one of my stay at the lovely overlook Tower 4. I asked my employers what I should write in this thing, but all they said to do was put whatever I wanted. According to them, no one really looks at this thing anyways because most of the data entry is done on a computer. This is more a symbolic gesture of unity with all of the past and future members that will join this humbling service.

It was a long drive out here. I think the last town I saw was 2 hours back the way I came. I had stopped for gas and got the feeling the locals weren't too keen on us being here. I don't know why they would be annoyed. You would think that someone sacrificing the better part of a year of their life to keep their woodlands safe, would get a little appreciation for that service. Instead, all I got was an old couple coming up to me and begging me to just "go back to where I came from."

When I got here, I was a little surprised at just how isolated the tower was from the rest of the world. The massive wooden structure was surrounded by an abnormally tall chain-link fence that greeted me as I drove up the winding road that acted like a driveway to a mansion. If that mansion was a 100 foot tall pedestal with a twenty-foot by twenty-foot studio apartment, I am not a fan that the bathroom is an outhouse that's located at the bottom of said hundred-foot tower plus a few feet. So, I guess I have to hope I don't eat some bad berries and end up with a case of the hershey squirts.

I think I'm going to end this entry here. I have a lot to unpack and I'm definitely gonna get my steps in today with the next few trips down to the jeep and back. At least I won't need to worry about cardio for the season. See ya tomorrow!

4/2/24

Ok I get I'm new to this type of job, but seriously and professionally, fuck those stairs! I mean honestly after the first trip or two, I was fine, but on numbers three and four, you should have heard the words coming out of my mouth. I wonder if you can build a solar powered elevator? Do you think I would get some kind of royalties if that gets invented? Screw it, I'm gonna trademark that shit. So to whoever is reading this, don't try and steal my idea.

Anyways, awesome ideas that will make me rich put aside, maybe I can bring my spirits up with just how superb this view is. The greenery of the tall pine trees over the rocky terrain going off into all directions and out of sight... there was just something about it that made the bullshit steps worth it. I think I saw a nice stream to the north that might be worth a visit and an outcropping of boulders to the west, just screaming to be climbed on.

While I was enjoying the scenery, I also received my first radio contact with Angela in Tower 3. She welcomed me and it was nice to hear another voice. I wasn't really prepared for the lack of interaction until last night, where the only thing to break through the sound the bugs were making was my poor attempt at karaoke without the backing tracks.

It seems that there is a fun little ritual for when we leave the tower at the end of our term. Our final sign off entries always end with **"Another one for the Books."** It seems to have been the norm for all the previous firewatch members going back to when the tower was first constructed up here.

Maybe if I ever get bored I'll read through some of the old entries. There are so many in here that it would be an activity on a slow night. I stopped on a few that mentioned some wild edibles nearby and a few recipes on how to prepare them. Hopefully I'll be eating pretty good out here. Learning to cook will help pass the time. Not like I can doom scroll my boredom away on my phone. They don't really warn you that you have zero signal, and the only thing the computer here is good for is basic report filing. The thing is so old, Moses could have done his rough draft of the ten commandments on it.

I think tomorrow, I'll go on a little adventure. Maybe Angela knows of a few fun trails to hike around here. I know I'm supposed to keep watch all the time, but if I go for a quick little jaunt through the woods in the morning after the first watch, I should be back around lunch time for the second. Don't tell anybody, it'll be our little secret.

4/3/24

Last night, something weird happened. I think there was an animal close to camp. Well, obviously there was an animal. I'm in the middle of a damn forest. However, what I mean is, last night, I was laying here listening to the surroundings and watching the stars. There was something about that situation that put into perspective just how small and insignificant we all are in the universe. The endless expanse of space above and the measurable, yet unbelievably large planet below that in comparison, I was nothing but a grain of sand on. But the size of earth compared to the entire universe was like me looking at an atom under an electron microscope.

I had always heard that the most memorable parts of the job were the views. It was so beautiful seeing the stars on such a clear night. The slight chill of the air with each breath was fresher than anything I had ever experienced in any city I had lived in. I had been so focussed on the sky that when I realized I had zoned out and snapped out of my thoughts, I had noticed that all the sounds of the forest seemed to have vanished.

I sat up and listened close, but it was like everything in a five mile radius decided to collectively shut up. The unusual silence went on for about five minutes. The whole time I strained to hear anything and I tried to see in the starlight, but even after flicking on the floodlamp and scanning the area, all that happened was the sounds of the bugs singing their song as the noises came back.

I don't know why, but even with all the bugs back, I couldn't help but wonder what was wandering around out there. It must have been a bear or something big to cause that many critters to all go mute. Needless to say, I double checked all the gates on the stairwell, just to be sure nothing came knocking.

I asked Angela if her tower got a visitor last night, but she figuratively waved it off with the excuse that it must have been a bear like I had thought. There were grizzlies in the area, so it made sense to me, but she said to watch myself, if I go for a walk. There was a rifle in the tower, and even though I was a shit shot, I feel I should maybe keep it close for any excursions.

Second note

I went for my first hike this morning. I decided to go see the little stream. It took about a half hour to get to it, but once I got there, it was a beautiful little brook that fed into a larger creek. Small waterfalls dotted the length. Little soaking pools at the top of each gave me thoughts of maybe coming out here to bathe. I mean, that's kind of bragging rights when picking up chicks. "Hey babe, I'm a real mountain man. I wash myself while standing at the top of waterfalls." Sure it sounds good to me now, but let's see what a few weeks of ice cold water will do. Hell, if it's cold enough, I might not need a woman. My junk might recess into me and give me an unwanted sex change.

While on my little adventure, I tried to see if I could find any tracks to indicate what caused the veil of silence last night, but the tracks I did find, all seemed to be pretty standard animals. Some rabbits, a few deer, and I did find a few that could have been a bear or a large mountain lion.

I did tighten my grip on my rifle at the thought that there was a mountain lion in the area. Once it set in that I wasn't the biggest badass out there, the instant feeling of being watched took over and I found myself coming back here to log my findings.

I let Angela know to keep an eye out, but she seemed kind of resigned to the fact that there are apex predators out here and that she could be eaten at any moment. If this is my first week, what's gonna happen the rest of the season?

4/4/24

Nothing much to report for today. I spent some time cleaning up the fenced in "yard" of this place. Going off the entries in the old log books, I've noticed that some of these people were a little paranoid. Can't say I blame them, but no one else is here.

I cleared some of the thorn bushes that looked almost as if planted along the base of the fence. The vines had grown through the links and were pretty tangled, but with some good ol' man handling, I managed to tear off quite a bit.

Don't tell anyone, but I felt real dumb doing that by hand. I did find some rusty lawn tools leaning up against the shed. They did make it easier to trim the weeds, but I'll have to make a note to request some newer ones in the next resupply drop.

I didn't hear anything from Angela today. She mentioned something yesterday about going to a special spot near what she called 'The Bluff.' Wasn't much to go off of. Maybe I should ask her about that. In case of an emergency.

4/5/24

I received a message from Angela late last night. She told me how she went to her special spot overlooking a small pond. She said it was a bit overgrown, but that she was happy to see that the local wildlife had been working its way in mowing it down and clearing some of the old brush.

I told her I had no clue what she meant and in my head pictured a bunch of cute woodland creatures in little vests, pushing lawn mowers and cutting trees with miniature chainsaws. She found that pretty funny.

I didn't tell her though, that she had kind of a cute giggle. Whoever gets posted here next, I hope you get to work with her. She helps pass the time out here.

4/6/24

I found a downed tree on one of the paths this morning. It looked to have been chewed through at the base of the trunk. Must have taken a small army of beavers with a contingent of woodpeckers in reserves to get through it. How did they plan to move it? I know beavers are pretty strong, but this tree was a good six feet around. I'm surprised I didn't hear it fall. Guess we have an answer to that question now.

I've already sent the request for the proper tools, a chainsaw and some fuel for it. There is no way in hell I'm going to cut through something that big with a hand saw. I'm not even close to the size of a lumberjack. Hell, I'm probably 150 pounds soaking wet with a crucifix in my pocket.

I'm gonna go look in the shed for something to mark the path with. I have to at least warn people. As rare as they may be out here.

Second note

I don't know which one of yall is the psycho that went nuts in the shed, but what the hell is the "Tall Camper?" The pictures were worn out or blurry, but yall are nuts. There was a whole crime web presentation, complete with red string, like some kind of shitty detective show. Or conspiracy theorists' basement.

I didn't wanna waste too much time looking through that today. Luckily, the caution tape and warning signs were out in the open, but I think I found something to keep me occupied. Nothing like the ramblings of a crazy person to pass the time.

4/7/24

Well, it's Sunday, which marks the last day of my first week... and look at me not going insane. I decided against telling Angela about what I found in the shed the other day. I figured I'll save it for one of those uneventful days that we need something to talk about and make fun of how crazy it is.

She said she saw something getting scared after going into a small cave. It was kind of a cute little hop before it snagged something and left. She didn't go investigate in case it was the mountain lion, bear critter that I found the tracks of. I found it to be a legit concern, but she just decided to go on and make some dark humor out of it.

Second note:

So, I said screw it to work after hiking back to that tree, marking it off and then while I'm walking back to base, I heard a loud series of cracks and another tree fell. It was a little close for comfort, but it dropped not too far off the trail. Still didn't mean I wasn't scared seeing it fall in my direction.

When it hit the ground a big plume of dirt and pine needles shot up from the ground in a cloud. I squinted to try and see through it, but I don't know if it was the light playing with my eyes, but I swear I saw a big shadow walking away. And I'm not talking like a bear-sized animal, I'm talking like, 10 feet tall with a human-like gate to its steps.

There was no way that was an animal. It had to have been just the way the light was reflecting or something. I think it's time to just relax for the night.

4/8/24

Ok, yall are insane. Whoever this Tall Camper is, it seems to be a hell of a running gag. I went down to the shed again and started rooting around down there. I found that there were things added throughout the decades this firewatch post has been in business. The first account, according to the wall, goes back to the early 1900s. I think it was in 1911.

Something about it being some kind of forest cryptid that isn't what it seems. People hearing voices of people they know are long dead, calling out to them from the darkness. It was nothing but poorly written ghost stories... and monster stories.

That's not the point, but what is, is that some of them went all out. The pictures looked like real polaroids. I even found an old 8mm camera hidden in a vintage and weathered carry case. I didn't find a projector in there, but finders keepers. I can always order one once I get back to the regular world.

Second note

Saw smoke coming from beyond the boulders in the west. It's about 3pm and I will be heading out to investigate.

Third note

That was weird. I went to check out the smoke and when I got to the rocky outcropping, I found a barricaded cave entrance. It looked almost like a mine, but it seemed too natural to be that.

I made a note on my map of the location and continued climbing up to get a better vantage point. When I reached the top I could still see smoke rising from a small clearing maybe a mile or so away.

I made a plan of action, but it was a very strange location to set up a place to camp. No matter where I looked, there didn't seem to be any easy way to access that area.

It took me about a half hour to make the trek, but when I got through the thick underbrush and crossed a few precarious cracks in the ground where the bedrock had split open god knows how long ago. I managed to make it to the source of the smoke, but something wasn't right.

I approached the lone fire pit, but there wasn't any smoke rising from it. There wasn't even a fire. As I approached, I felt no heat. I even touched the coals and they weren't hot. There hadn't been any rain, and even though the last smoke I saw was a half hour prior, there would still be some hot ash at least.

Here's the creepy part, next to the pit was a large flat stone with a crude map drawn on it with a piece of charcoal. What weirded me out was what was written on it.

There were a few circles and rough shapes indicating locations. When I matched it up with my map, the areas indicated things like the stream, a few caves, something that looked like the boulders, but the letters "YAH" matched up with where I was. There was another circle that matched with the tower's location. The letters "IAH" were jaggedly scribbled next to it.

The rock that this was all written on was huge, as well. I felt my stomach sink as the letters began to make sense. "YAH" means" "you are here." "IAH" means that someone was here, or at the tower while I was out.

When I got back to the fence, I spent a good portion of time looking over the grounds. There weren't many places for anyone to hide, but the few there were, I wanted to keep as much distance between them and me as possible.

I'm not gonna lie, I checked to be sure I had a round in the chamber before stepping through the gate. I had closed it before leaving, but it was wide open when I got back. I was terrified as I had to make the decision and I began the long ascent up the stairs.

Acting like some special forces asshole, doing my best to seem intimidating. When I reached the top, I stayed as low as possible, in case someone was in my cabin. My pulse was racing the closer I got to the doorway and I could almost smell the fear and sweat that was beginning to soak through my shirt as I tried to hide it. I heard something fall over inside and I took a few quiet deep breaths as I tried to psyche myself up.

I swung around and found myself face to face with a massive, terrifying squirrel eating out of a can of nuts it had knocked off the shelf. I felt relaxed for a minute as it stuffed its mouth full of nuts and scurried out an open window.

So yeah, my report today is about some creepy camper trying to scare me with a prank, and a fat squirrel ate my nuts. Great way to end a week.

4/9/24

That cheeky bitch. So I contacted Angela about the creepy map and how someone might be wandering the forest. I got all the way and was practically shaking with how unsettled I was before she burst out laughing. She drew the map and used a flair as the smoke.

She thought it was hilarious. I guess that's how she deals with the boredom, so pardon me while I go and change my shitty shorts.

Second note

I went back to the clearing knowing it was a joke now and not evidence of a creeper, but when I got back to the clearing I decided to take a picture of it with my phone. While reviewing the picture though, I noticed that the tower circle had been partially erased and now the rocks were circled with "IAH" marked next to it.

I could see the rocky bluff from where I was at and I turned to face them. As I focussed my camera on the peak, I wanted to get a picture of angela messing with me, but instead I saw someone unusually tall standing in the shadow of the trees. For a moment, I lowered my camera knowing I had her this time, but when I lifted my camera to get the shot, the tall shadow was gone.

Even when she was found out, she still wanted to mess with me. Instead of wasting the time trying to catch her, I just cleaned up the macabre prank and buried the fire pit. I would have to come up with a fun way to tag her back.

I decided to leave the map on the stone because if there are any lost hikers it might help them find a place close by. I made my way back here and thought I'd update. It would be a fun story if it did save someone someday.

Third note

Ok, I'm a little creeped out. I radioed her back and told her it was funny that she didn't stop the joke, but that it was losing its comedic value. She asked what I was talking about and I told her I saw her spying on me when I saw the change to the map.

The radio was silent for a few seconds, but her response seemed genuine. She told me she hadn't gone back to the clearing, let alone the outcropping. As is, the hike to my place from her tower is almost half a day's hike, and that her little prank was a full day round trip.

When I told her to quit joking and mentioned I'm not gonna fall for the Tall Camper story, if that's what she was gonna blame it on. All I got was a long silence.

After about a minute of me checking the radio to be sure it hadn't died. She finally got back to me and asked me where I had heard that story. I told her I found a whole shrine dedicated to it, not to mention the tower's log books. You would think I killed her dog with how quiet she was...

She started to panic and told me that I needed to stay in the tower for a few days. That it wasn't safe for me to be out of the perimeter fence. I tried to get a little more information, but she quickly ended the transmission and now I'm just sitting here with a gun in hand and a floodlight panning over the woods. I really hope this is just an elaborate joke. If it is, then I'm not laughing.

4/10/24

Everything was quiet last night. I mean that more in a literal sense than anything at the moment. I don't know what time it is, but it's still early in the morning. I should be hearing the birds chirping and all that shit. However, right now, it's just as quiet — if not quieter than the night last week.

There was a nice little warm front that moved through, and so I had left the window open. I went to the window and I swear I saw someone standing with their hands clasped around what looked like a map at the gate.

I watched them for a few minutes trying to figure out why they appeared so... weird looking. I couldn't put my finger on it, but in the low light and my half asleep state, something was both normal and abnormal at the same time with them.

Looking down at the stranger, I felt queasy as they turned their head to face up to look at me. Their face was blurry, as if someone had put a filter over it. I don't know how else to describe it.

I shouted down to them, asking if they needed any help. I turned on the spotlight, but before I could get a clear view, they tore the map in half and began walking away. Not like an adult though. It looked like they were walking like a baby taking its first steps. Their arms swayed in order to help keep their balance as they took disjointed steps into the darkness and vanished.

I don't remember going back to my bed or falling asleep again. I just woke up to my alarm and decided to make a note of the disturbing experience. It had to have just been a night terror or something. All the stress from today and Angela pulling her shit. It was a miracle I didn't have a worse hallucination.

4/14/24

I've been gone for days? The last thing I remember was walking back through the gate and coming up here after I went down to investigate where that creepy weirdo was standing last night, but all I could find was a few mismatched and confusing animal prints. A few looked like some sort of hoof marks with a rabbits toe beans. Another looked like some kind of dog, and the further I followed the weirder they got until eventually I found myself in the middle of nowhere.

I spun around having not paid attention to where I had come from. I planned to just follow the tracks back, but when I looked around, they were gone. All of them, even my own footprints seemed to have been wiped from the path.

I don't remember ever seeing the sun go down or rise. However, I do remember once I managed to get my thoughts back together, I could have sworn that I heard Angela's voice in the distance. Calling for me to follow. I started to walk in the direction I heard her and next thing I knew, I was back here. I felt like I had been walking for hours and I was covered in dirt.

I hailed her over the radio in order to thank her, but all I got was a panicked voice in return. She went off on how she's been trying to get a hold of me for three days. I thought she was joking until I checked the date on the computer. I don't know what I'm gonna tell the office, but when I told Angela about what happened she told me not to worry and that she would handle it.

What is she not telling me?

4/15/24

I couldn't sleep last night. The animals and bugs were out in full force and horny as hell. The noise was deafening, but it was definitely welcome. I spent the day trying to remember what happened. Maybe it was just a dream? Maybe something I ate caused some sort of short term coma?

I don't know... maybe that's why I can't sleep right now? In all honesty, I'm finding that this log is probably the one thing keeping my mind focussed. I went through the older ones and whoever this Tall Camper is, seems to fit the description of my hallucination. The reason the thorn bushes were allowed to get entangled was to keep it out. The watcher wrote that it acted like a natural barbed wire.

Alan was his name. He said that he had gone to search for a lead from one of the other towers. They reported smoke from one of the open fields and so he discovered a small bonfire. Seemed like the joke was going on all the way back then, too.

He went on to describe that when he arrived at the waypoint, he discovered the smoking little ring of rocks, but when he stomped it out, he says that he looked up to the treeline and saw a giant of a man. Easily 10 or 12 feet tall. Its limbs folded in front of it as if holding something. Its body was thin, but its skin seemed to have been grown in the shape of clothing. Its head was oblong, like a vertical football.When it faced him, a slit formed and when it peeled back, it looked like it was a throw rug being rolled to the sides. It began to spread its arms until whatever it appeared to be holding began to emit a glowing light in a crooked line.

He reported that once the hands parted, he found himself in a towering inferno. Everything that surrounded him was engulfed in an uncontrolled blaze. He had no idea how to describe it other than a scene pulled straight from the depths of hell and wrapped around him. When he looked back at the strange being, he couldn't tell if it was an angel or a demon. Its arms rose slowly and split into thin slices forming into bloodied wings with feathers of flesh.

He went on to say that as whatever the beast was, that as it bent down to charge at him. Its wings gently lowered to the ground and the fire seemed to snuff out as soon as it sprang to its feet.

He found himself dodging through the trees and hurdling the boulders in his path before tripping into a thicket of thorn bushes.

He said that when he fell, he could hear the crippled steps of the affront to nature. He prayed for god to save him and when the thin fleshy skin of the beast tried to reach through, the tiny spikes tore at its skin causing it to run off in pain and annoyance.

Since that incident, he began to only leave the tower when absolutely necessary and that he had transplanted as many thorn bushes as he could to surround the tower.

He appears to have survived the season, because he signed off his last log as all the others.

"Another one for the books."

That entry was from the fifties. I think I'm gonna read through some more of these. I told Angela that I need a few days to recover and deal with how I lost three days. I must be going crazy.

4/17/24

I lost track of time again. It's two in the morning and I spent all day reading through these logs and I'm sensing a pattern. It almost seems like a lot of them had been censored with a thick black marker. It only seemed to make it to a certain point and then it was just random ramblings scribbled across the pages. "DON'T LOOK AT IT!" "DON'T ACKNOWLEDGE IT!" And a bunch of variations of that type of warnings. The one that was most prominent though was "DON'T TRUST THE VOICES!"

So many times he repeated it, covering as much as they could to keep me or whoever else from reading it. What voices?

I was getting invested now in whatever this mystery was. If for nothing else, I want answers.

4/20/24

It came back again. I did what the note said. I did my best to ignore it, but all it did was move around the fence, doing its best to get into my line of sight. I tried to call Angela, but she was ignoring me or was busy. I am leaning more towards the first option. Of course she would be. The new guy sending weird messages about some creepy monster camper. Maybe she called the rangers? Yeah, maybe she doesn't think I'm crazy. Maybe she wants to help me.

Second note

I went down and measured the height of the fence. It's eight feet tall, when I saw that asshole staring up at me. It had to have been a good two or three feet higher for me to see it as I did. That's just not possible for a person to be that tall. Let alone an animal.

Third note

I swear I saw something while out on patrol again. I had to get out, but this rifle isn't leaving my side. I don't give a fuck. I found a grizzly bear carcass. A whole ass fucking grizzly. Whatever got to it dissembowled it like it was a fucking squirrel and stapled it to a tree with its own bones! Who the hell — or what the hell — could even do that to something that size?

I went to my jeep and wanted to get the hell out of here, but when I got to it, something had flipped it over and tore out the drive shaft. Something clearly didn't want me to leave and it made it pretty fucking clear it had the power to make me.

I ran up to the radio, at this point I don't care if the bitch thinks I'm crazy, I'm getting the hell out of here.

4/21/24

Went on patrol along the ridge. Such a beautiful day. Nothing to report.

4/22/24
Went on paTROLl, nothing To report.

4/23/24

Found some campers with an unauthorized fire. REMOVED THEM FROM THE AREA...

4/24/24

Troubled CAMPER seems to be lost. FOUND HIM and helped him to A TRAIL.

4/25/24
CLEARED DEBRIS FROM CAVE ENTRANCE.

4/26/24

CLEARED THE DOWNED TREE FROM THE PATH.

4/30/24
BEEN TRACKING AN ANIMAL THAT APPEARS
TO BE RABID. I FOUND IT, BUT CAN'T GET TO IT!

5/13/24

I've been running for so long. I went to radio Angela and all I got was static. The few words that did make it through were from my fucking parents. They've been dead for five fucking years! How could I hear them? I abandoned the tower and just ran.

I don't know where the hell I was, but I swear that creepy fuck was watching me! I ran back here to grab a few things and I'm gonna hide someplace that isn't here. It knows where I'm at, but if I keep moving it can't follow me now can it?

5/15/24

What are some of these entries? I was gone for ten days?
When the hell were these entered? Was someone in my tower?
I never found any campers. What the hell is going on here?

5/18/24

I'm back at the tower, I spent the night keeping an eye out for that monstrosity. I got a hold of Angela, though, and she seemed to be trying to explain it away as nothing more than I was getting some sort of isolation sickness or some shit. I know what I saw.

She kept telling me it's all in my head and that there isn't anything but some stupid campers and animals out here. That my lapses in time were just my brain compensating for the boredom of being alone. It's not some made up crap like she is making it sound. This is real! I may not be sane to her, but I know I'm not crazy.

I tried to tell her that I've seen it with my own eyes. That there are records of it all over the tower. I begged her to even come here to see it for herself, but by the end of the conversation, she told me that enough was enough and that she was calling to have me replaced.

It wasn't what I wanted, but at least if someone came to relieve me then this wouldn't be my problem anymore. It seems to me the only things that are true are what's written in this book.

I hear it outside the fence. I don't want to look at it, it might see me. I wired the gate shut, but who knows if that'll hold. I don't have a clue if that thing can just tear it apart if it really wanted to.

5/31/24

Forest Ranger O'Hanlon, Tower 4, firewatch member Jacob Brunstein has been found alive. He was not on site when we arrived, but were informed via radio that Jacob may have been in one of the caves in the area.

We discovered Mr. Brunstein in cave number five. He had somehow destroyed the gate and warning signs and blockaded himself inside a small hole. He didn't come willingly and appeared to have been held up there for several days, mumbling to himself about how "The Tall Camper" was stalking him. How the voices were coming from this camper and that it couldn't get him there.

We had to subdue the individual using a security blanket. However, we did extract him from his hidey hole and got him on the helicopter.

The new member is to be arriving in a few days.
"ANOTHER ONE FOR THE BOOKS"

8/17/24

Do you see the issue here? What he mentioned in the shed was what I have been building all this time. A web of clues. Ways to avoid it, but he survived, and I might survive, too. Clearly it was something I wrote down for him that saved his life, or at the very least, pointed him in the right direction. right?

The detail that he went into, the...

I just got a call from Angela, she told me there is smoke coming from... no... ok, I'm going to have to come back to this. I think I just had a revelation. I have to finish letting him know. Maybe if I write it down now it will appear for him. It's so obvious.

6/3/24

Hey! It's Brittni. I just dropped in today, and I gotta say, this place is soooooo beautiful! I mean at first I was like, kinda short notice, but the big boss-man said it would be greatly appreciated, and he also told me I would get a hefty bonus for the inconvenience. So I said, "Yes daddy!" and here we are.

I don't know what happened to the last person that was here, but given the state of this place, which is just, EW! They clearly didn't respect this place. Guess it's for the best that they went a little cray cray.

I already radioed in and such a cute voiced little chica named Angela replied. OMG, she onboarded me, and she was just the best! Well, anyways! I think that's all for today! I'll log in you tomorrow, Bye!!!

6/4/24

So I saw the CUTEST!!! BUNNY!!! Today. I was hiking up to this little outcropping to do my morning yoga, and it was just hip hoppin along. It was so adorbs, with its little squished in bread loaf of a body and its little wiggling lips as it nibbled the leaves of one of the bushes.

I tried to sneak up to it, but my foot broke a branch and it scampered off with its little booty jiggling. It didn't look as chonky as a pet rabbit, but it was deff eating well.

Note

There were some campers that I could see from my little perch. They were all getting set up down in a clearing. They looked like they were setting up a tent. I think it was a mom, dad and kid. I guess I have to actually do something tonight and be sure they don't burn the place down.

Okay, guess I'll post on here tomorrow! BYE!!!

6/5/24

So, Anggie just informed me that there is no shower here! Totally gross, I can't believe that was left out of the job description. I'm gonna be so nasty if I can't take a bath. She told me there was a creek about a mile from the tower that will have to "suffice," whatever that means.

So I'll check back after I get my clean on.

Note

That water is so cold! I'm glad I brought my bikini. My nips were hard enough to cut glass by the time I was done. While I was there getting lathered up, I felt like some perv was watching me from behind a tree. As hot as that is sometimes, it wasn't on my list for this summer.

I stopped by the bluff again to check up on that family. It was pretty funny, the dad seemed to be trying to teach the kid how to set up a portable grill and failing horribly. It was a highlight given the feeling of a peeping tom while trying to be clean.

I remember asking Angie about where she goes, and she said she goes all natural for these five to seven months. I actually gagged at the thought of how smelly her lookout is. She said that when she goes home, her tub looks like a german shepard stuck in an oil slick, after her first shave and bath in all that time. GAG!

I can't even talk about it right now. I still gotta eat. Okay BYEEEE!!!

6/8/24

PINE CONES ARE NOT A GOOD SUBSTITUTE FOR TOILET PAPER! I can't believe I forgot to pack it in my backpack. I wanted to explore for a little bit and I thought I was only gonna be out for a few hours today.

Instead, I somehow got turned around and ended up a little lost. Luckily I brought a compass, but when nature called, it was a photo finish to get my shorts down. The nightmare really began when I opened my pack and low and behold, I forgot the one thing I brought a ton of back at the tower. Now, I can't tell if my ass is bleeding or not because the damn cones were already slightly red to begin with. Odd color for them, but that's not the point!

I staggered from my little chili-hole and found myself in the clearing that the family I saw the other day had been in. I was on the other side of the hill from them, but at least I had a heading.

I'm honestly surprised that I didn't hear them when I was avoiding them. I didn't want to freak them out or anything, but thinking about it now, it was more creepy to be all stalkerish. Not like they would ever know.

Note

So, kinda freaky, I think I'll have to contact tech support, this dinosaur of a computer is saying a few days have passed, which is ridiculous. I wish the old bastards would just update these places. Ya know – keep up with the times.

Looks like it's time for some nice tea and to watch the sunset.

Note #2

I'm guessing today is just a whirlwind of weird stuff. I just got back from having my tea on the outcropping. The hike is nice this time of day so I went up to enjoy a hot drink while watching the sunset on the rock outcropping, and I brought my binoculars to check up on how that family was doing.

I hadn't seen so much as a poof of smoke from the grill they had set up in the last day or so, but when I looked over in their direction, the entire camp was gone. The weird part was that there was someone standing in the middle of the small field, on top of the little hill.

I tried to focus in, but when the binoculars went fuzzy as I tried to focus on the camper, they seemed to disappear into the fiery glare of the setting sun in the west. It was probably just my eyes, the bright on my left and dark on the right, I must have just seen a shadow.

Ok, well, since we have had our daily dose of weirdness. I think I'm only gonna update this thing when something interesting happens. Okay, BYE!!!

6/19/24

This bathing in a creek thing is kind of growing on me now. OH! Can you imagine if I found some sort of healing crystals in the water and it made me more beautiful?

Anyways, I'm entering this in because I saw another camper today. They were way down the path, but I went for a walk on a trail I hadn't noticed before that went down into this cute little oasis of a ravine. But as I was checking out the cute little animals and looking at the flowers that were in bloom, I looked up at the exit and saw a large person standing at the edge of one of the cliffs.

They weren't looking at me. In fact, whoever they were, they were staring off into the distance. Not wanting to be rude, I shouted up to them to say hi, but instead of saying anything, their head just turned, and my eyes must have been playing tricks on me, because their face looked to have been tattooed on. Like someone wearing a mosquito net or a nylon mask with a face printed on it. When it looked down at me, it stared at me with those uncanny eyes for a solid, like, 30 seconds while smiling. They then turned back to whatever they were looking at before and walked away. But they must have been injured because the gestures their head was making made it look like they had MS.

So brave of them to be out here and powering through their disability. Maybe he was in a fire? That would explain the freaky face. Whateves, maybe they were moot? Mute? That thing where you can't talk.

Well, more importantly, they gave me some creeper vibes, so I decided that that was enough naturing for today and that it was time to head back here.

Note #1

Why is it so quiet tonight? I couldn't sleep. So I guess you get the ramblings until I pass out. Everytime I close my eyes, all I see is that weirdo's face. The more I tried to get a clearer image in my mind though, the more distorted it became. It was like the shapes were there, but it wasn't real. It was like it was made of flesh. I kept waking up and eventually gave up on the whole sleep situation.

Note #2

I saw that weirdo down in the yard! What do I do, what do I do?! They weren't doing anything, but the fact that they were standing there in the middle of the night and not doing anything. I'm kicking myself for not double checking the gate lock.

Note #3

FUCK! I can hear them walking up the stairs. It doesn't sound like feet on wood. They sound staggered. Oh god are they drunk? Are they going to try and... no no no no no!

If this is my last message, please come looking for me. No! This isn't where I'm going to die!

6/22/24

I tried to make it to Anngie's. I don't know where I am. I saw it, I fucking saw it. That's not a person. Not anymore or if it ever was.

I heard the footsteps stop and get quieter, I thought it was leaving, I thought it was CLEAR!

No, I had to do the stupid white girl thing and look. It was quiet and there was no reason for me to think it wasn't. All I did was peek my head out and I didn't see it. I stupidly walked down the balcony and by the time I got to the stairs, I heard it drop down. Its hands split apart, there was a flash of bright light with an unholy sound that was like listening to an elk howl in pain while children giggled. Then I found myself running in the woods. I still had this stupid book, but now I have no clue where the hell I am or how I got here...

Note #1

I've been walking for hours now. I can hear the rescue workers calling for me, but no matter how fast I run or how loud I scream for their attention, they only seem to get farther away.

I don't recognize any of these paths. This is not cool. I just wanted a relaxing summer with no bullshit!

6/29/24

WHAT THE FUCK IS GOING ON?! I just woke up in my cot. I remember covering myself with some branches and leaves in order to try and stay warm through the night, but somehow I ended up here. It must have all been some horrible dream?

I went to each of the windows and saw that it was sometime mid-day. The sun was bright and I could feel the warmth of its rays kissing my skin. I looked down and all around me the forest lay in ruin. Burnt to the roots of the oldest trees. Along my fence all the woodland creatures I had grown so attached to, were strung up and sewn into the links of it. The e sound of the torrential wind was filled with the agony of their crucifixions. I looked up to see the creature, the awkward proportions of its body, levitated in a ring of fire above the destruction.

Its cold black eye gently exited the fleshy tomb that was its head, the nerve still attached. The very ground I was standing on began to tear away in chunks and was dragged into the inky abyss of the black hole.

There was no place to run, the very world was drained away, all that remained was the light in the darkness before I found myself screaming from within the black orb, and the light itself slowly vanished into the ether.

I woke up to the sound of Anggie's panicked voice shouting for me over the radio. She said that there was smoke coming from somewhere close to my tower. I tried to tell her that I didn't even know what day it was, that something wasn't right.

She told me that I needed to calm down. Who the hell did she think she was? When I asked her why she didn't seem concerned about not hearing from me for days, she told me I must be crazy because she's been talking to me the whole time.

I don't know who she's been talking to, but it wasn't me. I hope this smoke is nothing.

7/5/24

I don't know what it is about this tower, but this is Forest Ranger Skudlark. Watch tower member, Britani Esmond's remains have been found. Unsure of what got her, but it was clearly some sort of animal attack. She appears to have been out here for weeks. Her body was torn to pieces, her muscles looked to have been pulled right off the bone, not even eaten. Scorch marks were present on the dried out bones. As if they had been set on fire from the inside out. Angela said that she was told she was going to be investigating a small fire in the general area where we discovered her remains.

What I don't understand is that her last entry was only a few days ago. Could someone be attacking these kids? I may need to put in a request.

"Another one for the Books"

8/31/24

Who the hell was in my tower? Why was Brittani's file stapled in. And why does it say I found her body? I was never part of the crews to find these people.

I've been running for days. I don't know how I got into the western woods. I was gathering up some more thorn bushes, I only have to survive one more night, and I am not going to die on the last day. My ride out will be tomorrow and I scribbled my warnings for the boy. I only hope that he understands.

I don't plan to leave this tower until I hear the chopper land.

Note 1

I can hear her voice... I can hear all of her voices. It's all been a game for it, all a ruse in order to feed off those it deems as trespassers in its lands. *WE ARE* trespassers on its lands. I don't know what womb birthed that creature, but it is not from here.

I pulled the power from the radio, but the voices still came, it was never on to begin with. Everythings gone quiet and I know it's near. It stops the sound not because of its presence, but because it is the sound. There hasn't been a real animal here all this time, all the sightings were just... just all the creatures that came to its land. It has devoured every insect, every threat.

To whoever finds this, reads it, if I don't make it to the pick up tomorrow, follow the rules in the shed.

Don't bother it!

Don't acknowledge it!

Ignore the voices!

She isn't real!

We are the books...

9/1/24

"ANOTHER ONE FOR THE BOOKS" "ANOTHER ONE FOR THE BOOKS" "ANOTHER ONE FOR THE BOOKS" "ANOTHER ONE FOR THE BOOKS" "ANOTHER ONE FOR THE BOOKS" "ANOTHER ONE FOR THE BOOKS" "ANOTHER ONE FOR THE BOOKS" "ANOTHER ONE FOR THE BOOKS" "ANOTHER ONE FOR THE BOOKS" "ANOTHER ONE FOR THE BOOKS" "ANOTHER ONE FOR THE BOOKS" "ANOTHER ONE FOR THE BOOKS" "ANOTHER ONE FOR THE BOOKS" "ANOTHER ONE FOR THE BOOKS" "ANOTHER ONE FOR THE BOOKS" "ANOTHER ONE FOR THE BOOKS" "ANOTHER ONE FOR THE BOOKS"

Note 1

They are satisfied for another season. Selection for next year will begin soon.

Don't miss out!

Visit the website below and you can sign up to receive emails whenever Steven Bazydlo publishes a new book. There's no charge and no obligation.

https://books2read.com/r/B-A-IUDS-OXMIF

BOOKS 2 READ

Connecting independent readers to independent writers.